MW01234771

TRAITS

WHAT EVERY EMPLOYER IS LOOKING FOR

EZRA "E.G." HARVIN

authorHOUSE®

AuthorHouse™
1663 Liberty Drive
Bloomington, IN 47403
www.authorhouse.com
Phone: 1-800-839-8640

Published by AuthorHouse   1/2/2015

ISBN: 978-1-4969-4388-0 (sc)
ISBN: 978-1-4969-4387-3 (e)

Library of Congress Control Number: 2014917437

ENDORSEMENTS

"I have known E. G. Harvin for over [fifteen] years. It's because of his integrity and overall character that I agreed to read this book.

I want everyone to know that as an educator for my entire life, I have never read or seen a book that is more needed in our junior high and high school curricula. It absolutely can prepare our children for the real world in a way that is nothing short of phenomenal."

> —Dr. Ed Eissey, teacher, coach, first principal of Palm Beach Gardens High School; president of Palm Beach Community College for [nineteen] years; National Board of Governors, St. Jude Children's Research Hospital since 1974

"This book, created for the benefit of students, was written in an easy-to-follow, common-sense manner. I plan to use it as a guide in my classes, because it touches upon key and important life skills.

With deep appreciation and respect for writing such a fine, thought provoking book."

> —Professor Maria Garcia, associate professor English and reading, Palm Beach State College

"I have known E. G. Harvin for many years, both as a friend and as a leader in our church.

I truly believe that this work will and should be a powerful training tool for any business. E. G. touches on good business practices through good work habits, moral habits, and fairness to the employee and employer alike.

This book is a tool that I would have used, as required reading for my management team in all eleven stores I supervised."

—Paul T. Machtel, retired vice president
and store director, Jacobson's

"This book, *Traits*, is a nice easy read that has much impact in it.

As a principal of a large elementary public school, I see this book as a guide through all grade levels providing good things to live by! I also would believe *all* will benefit by reading this book.

For children, students, young adults, and those looking to rebound in life, this is a *must* read!"

—Jeffrey A. Pegg, elementary school
principal, Palm Beach County Schools

"I have known E. G. for [fifty] years and I can truly say he is a man who not only talks the talk but walks the walk.

His book is a compilation of the teachings that many of us learned in our homes, churches, and extended families in our communities. Sadly, today that is not the case. With both parents working, or with many homes managing with a single parent, the teaching of these traits is barely skimmed. It is an easy read and organized in a way that is simple to follow.

Thank you, E. G. for providing an easy-to-follow road map through the traits many of us grew up with! This is a must have for companies as well as schools."

—Beverly W. Carroll, retired principal and school administrator, Wayne County Public Schools; Goldsboro, North Carolina

"Ideas are powerful! They fuel the engine of creativity and production in the business world. E. G. Harvin has identified ideas that every employee needs to succeed in business and life. People are hired for skill sets and fired for their personalities. Mastering the ideas in *Traits* will unlock the unlimited potential in everyone."

—Dale Hedrick, Hedrick Brothers Construction Company

DID YOU KNOW?

In our country there are seven major centers of influence, also known as the *Seven Mountains of Culture*: **the Family Mountain, the Religious Mountain, the Education Mountain, the Media Mountain, the Arts and Entertainment Mountain, the Government Mountain, and the Business Mountain.**

All young and older adults alike will have an opportunity as well as a responsibility, to bring a positive influence to one or more of these Seven Mountains.

As you climb the mountains in your life, never forget you will be remembered far more for what you give back than for your fame and fortune.

Master the *traits* within this book and they will take you to the top of any mountain you attempt to climb.

PREFACE

If the material within the pages of this one little book, even in part, is retained and put into practice, it will always enable people to be better and more productive.

The material, although primarily designed to benefit employees, and thus companies, also holds true for any business or personal relationship.

Two Thoughts to Ponder:

1. What subject taught in our high schools today provides more assistance, more value, to our young people than these thirty-two traits?

2. What company would not be thrilled to interview a young man or woman that brought this book, with all traits signed, to an interview?

ACKNOWLEDGMENTS

As the author, I would personally like to thank two very close friends, Art Peacock and Nancy Talbert Smith, for their assistance in proof reading my book and for their overall encouragement.

FROM THE AUTHOR

Yes, it's true. *Knowing* the material in this book is very valuable; however, *possessing* the outlined traits is ultimately more valuable.

Think about it, just for a moment; isn't it logical that if you are being interviewed for a company position or you already have a position, that you are much more likely to obtain the position or keep the position if you are bringing value to the company that fellow interviewees or employees don't possess?

If you wish to have success and excel in a career or relationship of any kind, you have no option but to master the traits outlined in this book.

Situation: You have applied for a position at a local business. Your résumé was reviewed, and you have received a phone call to come in and meet Mr. Jones, the person who does all the hiring for this small but rapidly growing company. You already know, or at least should assume, that other qualified people will be applying for the same position. The questions become: Why should Mr. Jones hire you? What will you bring to the table that is superior to the other applicants?

Everything being equal, this one statement will make all the difference: "Mr. Jones, with all due respect, I can bring things to your company that cannot be taught. I am ambitious, dependable, honest, hard-working, and I have a great attitude."

These qualities and all others that you will need to make your personal and business dreams come true are in this one little book.

Note: The attributes that you promise Mr. Jones you will bring to his company must be true; they must be ingrained in you and be part of who you are. Otherwise, they may get you into a position in which you will not be able to succeed.

Have a great career, and may all your relationships, both business and personal, be real and genuine.

Have a great life! It's completely in your hands.

Ezra "E. G." Harvin

CONTENTS

Family Traits

Chapter 1
Personal Traits

Integrity
Honesty
Humility
Patience
Self-Control
Correct Motives
Positive Attitude
Sense of Humor

The Personal Trait of having
Integrity

"I always try to do the right thing, even when no one is watching."

Integrity is the ability to accept one's past choices and actions and act in accordance with one's inner values. **Integrity** is choosing your thoughts and actions based on personal, ingrained, honest values, and not on personal gain.

It is better to be a poor man who walks with **Integrity** than a rich man who is crooked in his ways.

Always be more concerned with your character than your reputation. Your character is who you really are, while your reputation is merely what others believe you to be.

Remember, honesty and **Integrity** are absolutely essential for success in all areas of your life. The good news is that they don't have to be learned; they are simply choices. Your word must be your bond. Very simply put, if you say you're going to do something, do it. If you start something, finish it.

People of **Integrity** do the right thing even if no one else does, not because they think it will change the world, but because they refuse to be changed by the world. *Knowledge* is being aware of the right path to take; **Integrity** is taking the right path.

Advantages of having *Integrity*:
1. You will be respected by others.
2. You will be given the benefit of the doubt.

3. You will feel good about the person you see in the mirror.

A thought to ponder: You can obtain much fame and fortune and be a failure, as success without *Integrity* is failure.

On a scale of 1 to 10, 10 being perfect, I give myself a: ____

I have read, understand, and believe the points as outlined for the personal trait of having *Integrity*.

_____   _____
Signature   Date

Personal thoughts regarding
the Trait of having *Integrity*

Why I gave myself this point value:

_____

_____

_____

_____

_____

_____

_____

What I can do to raise my point value:

_____

_____

_____

_____

_____

_____

_____

Why I believe this trait is important to have in my life:

_____

_____

_____

_____

_____

_____

_____

The Personal Trait of having
Honesty

"I've discovered that **Honesty** is always the best policy."

The greatest advantage of speaking the truth is that you never have to remember what you said.

In life we always have the choice of two roads: the road of **Honesty** and the road of dishonesty. Many times, the shortsighted take the road of dishonesty while the wise take the road of **Honesty**. The wise know the truth and value of helping others; they know that when they help others that they in turn are helped.

Character always overshadows wealth, and trust is a priceless asset.

Being **Honest** may not get you a lot of friends, but it'll always get you the right ones.

In order to succeed, you will need for your customers or fellow employees to see you as reliable, dependable, credible, open, and **Honest**.

There are four very important words in life: *love, **Honesty**, truth,* and *respect*. If these are not part of your life and who you are, you have nothing.

Personal and business relationships take a lot of practice, sacrifice, pain, forgiveness, and **Honesty**. Like anything of value in life, achieving good relationships will never be easy.

In a relationship, **Honesty** and trust are a must! If they are not present, an individual is not capable of love. So if you can't be **Honest**, stay single.

Advantages of having _Honesty_:
1. Others will know that you are trustworthy.
2. You will be well respected.
3. You will have many true friends.

A thought to ponder: An _Honest_ comment never needs to be amended.

On a scale of 1 to 10, 10 being perfect, I give myself a: _____

I have read, understand, and believe the points as outlined for the personal trait of having **Honesty**.

_____   _____
Signature   Date

Personal thoughts regarding
the Trait of having *Honesty*

Why I gave myself this point value:

_____

_____

_____

_____

_____

_____

_____

What I can do to raise my point value:

_____

_____

_____

_____

_____

_____

_____

Why I believe this trait is important to have in my life:

_____

_____

_____

_____

_____

_____

_____

The Personal Trait of having
Humility

"I try not to think of myself more highly than others."

True **Humility** is staying teachable, regardless of how much you already know. **Humility** is the opposite of pride. Pride causes you to fail, while **Humility** promotes your success. Greatness is not found in power, wealth, or position; it's discovered in character and **Humility**.

Being **Humble** means recognizing that we are not on earth to see how important we can become but to see how much difference we can make in the lives of others.

True **Humility** is intelligent self-respect that keeps us from thinking too highly of ourselves. It keeps us down-to-earth and reminds us how much more we can learn, even if others believe we know it all. To be the greatest is an aspiration for the immature, but is completely irrelevant to a person of **Humility**.

Humility is the knowledge and wisdom of accepting the fact that you can be wrong.

Have enough confidence to believe that you can solve any problem, and enough **Humility** to understand that some of your initial ideas may be wrong. Have enough **Humility** to listen to others who may have some good ideas of their own. **Humility** always involves being a good listener.

Advantages of having *Humility*:
1. You are appreciated by others.
2. You are known as a person with concern for others.

3. You are known as one who gathers all the facts before making bold statements.

A thought to ponder: *Humble* people are respected, not because of what they know, but because of who they are.

On a scale of 1 to 10, 10 being perfect, I give myself a: _____

I have read, understand, and believe the points as outlined for the personal trait of having **Humility.**

_____   _____

Signature   Date

Personal thoughts regarding
the Trait of having *Humility*

Why I gave myself this point value:

_____
_____
_____
_____
_____
_____
_____

What I can do to raise my point value:

_____
_____
_____
_____
_____
_____
_____

Why I believe this trait is important to have in my life:

_____
_____
_____
_____
_____
_____
_____

The Personal Trait of having
Patience

"Once I realized that I wasn't perfect, it became much easier to have *Patience* with others."

Patience is not the ability to wait, but the ability to keep a good attitude while doing so. Two things define you: your *Patience* when you have nothing and your attitude when you have everything.

Patience is a form of wisdom. It demonstrates that we understand and accept the fact that sometimes things must unfold in their own time.

Good things come to those who believe, but better things come to those who are *Patient*. Sometimes, no matter how much you want something to happen, all you can do is wait. Usually, waiting with *Patience* is the most difficult part.

Strength doesn't lie in carrying heavy loads— a horse can do that. Strength lies in being *Patient*.

Being *Patient* is never caused by a lack of ambition. Having *Patience* simply lets others know that good things often take time to evolve.

Showing *Patience* in a moment of anger saves a thousand moments of regret. When you're tempted to lose *Patience* with someone, think about a time when someone has been *Patient* with you.

Advantages of having *Patience*:
1. Others will know that you have concern for them.
2. You are never anxious and always content.
3. It's a way of letting others know that they matter.

A thought to ponder: In order to favorably coexist with others, impatience is not an option.

On a scale of 1 to 10, 10 being perfect, I give myself a: ____

I have read, understand, and believe the points as outlined for the personal trait of having *Patience*.

_____   _____
          Signature   Date

Personal thoughts regarding
the Trait of having *Patience*

Why I gave myself this point value:

_____

_____

_____

_____

_____

_____

_____

What I can do to raise my point value:

_____

_____

_____

_____

_____

_____

_____

Why I believe this trait is important to have in my life:

_____

_____

_____

_____

_____

_____

_____

The Personal Trait of having
Self-Control

"I always say that uncontrolled emotions are juvenile."

Anyone can criticize, condemn, and complain, but it takes character and **Self-Control** to be understanding and forgiving.

A person who has **Self-Control** over his emotions has great power over those who don't. **Self-Control** is a key factor in achieving success. We can't control everything in life, but we can definitely control ourselves.

One thing is very true: if we don't take control of our emotions, our emotions will take control of us. We cannot always control what happens to us, but we can control our attitude toward what happens, and in that, we will be mastering change rather than allowing it to master us. In business, you will never be given an opportunity to have control of others if you can't control yourself.

Self-Control is realizing that you have control over your mind and the words that come out of your mouth. Realizing this will deliver great strength, as well as an advantage in dealing with others.

If someone or something is causing your blood pressure to rise, do your best to stay calm, even if you feel like throwing a fit. Acting out won't help anything. It might just put you in a bad light and you could end up regretting it in a big way. Remember—work on staying calm, and trust that others aren't out to get you.

There is no greatness without **Self-Control**. Development that does not include personal constraint will only guarantee mediocrity.

Advantages of having *Self-Control*:
1. You will always make better decisions.
2. You will have a life of contentment.
3. Your decision-making process will be superior to most.

A thought to ponder: The tongue is a very small muscle, but it can inflict much damage.

On a scale of 1 to 10, 10 being perfect, I give myself a: _____

I have read, understand, and believe the points as outlined for the personal trait of having ***Self-Control***.

_____   _____
　　　　Signature　　　　　　　　　　　　　　Date

Personal thoughts regarding
the Trait of having **Self-Control**

Why I gave myself this point value:

_____
_____
_____
_____
_____
_____
_____

What I can do to raise my point value:

_____
_____
_____
_____
_____
_____
_____

Why I believe this trait is important to have in my life:

_____
_____
_____
_____
_____
_____
_____

The Personal Trait of having
Correct Motives

"I am interested in making a lot of money because there are a lot of people that I would then be able to help."

A **Correct Motive** cannot sanction a bad action. Bad motives can never produce good results.

A great and noble **Correct Motive** is to leave the world a better place than you found it. **Correct Motives** always take into account the impact that actions will have on others.

A **Correct Motive** for owning a company is to provide a product or service that can improve the lives of others. A **Correct Motive** for being an employee is to assist the owner in achieving the same goals. A **Correct Motive** for being in a relationship is to love and serve the one to whom you are committed.

A **Correct Motive** is not the end result, but is always involved when the end result is good. For any goal that you may have in life, or for anything that you may wish to accomplish, you should always ask yourself the question, "Do I have **Correct Motives**?"

Advantages of having *Correct Motives*:
1. You will be trusted by others.
2. Others will know that you have their best interest in mind.
3. You will always produce results of which you can be proud.

A thought to ponder: With *Correct Motives* you may, from time to time, need to start over, but you will never fail or be considered a failure.

On a scale of 1 to 10, 10 being perfect, I give myself a: _____

I have read, understand, and believe the points as outlined for the personal trait of having *Correct Motives*.

_____   _____

      Signature   Date

Personal thoughts regarding
the Trait of having **Correct Motives**

Why I gave myself this point value:

_____
_____
_____
_____
_____
_____
_____

What I can do to raise my point value:

_____
_____
_____
_____
_____
_____
_____

Why I believe this trait is important to have in my life:

_____
_____
_____
_____
_____
_____
_____

The Personal Trait of having a
Positive Attitude

"Don't know about you, but my glass is always half-full."

A **Positive Attitude** means thinking about achieving, believing you will achieve, and acting as if you have already achieved. With a **Positive Attitude** come strength, energy, motivation, and initiative.

A **Positive Attitude** means expecting more than you should and knowing that you will accomplish more than others expect.

There may be little difference between two people, but that little difference can make a big difference. The little difference is attitude. The big difference is whether it is positive or negative.

A negative thinker sees difficulty in every opportunity, while a person with a **Positive Attitude** always sees opportunity in the midst of difficulties. A **Positive Attitude** causes a chain reaction of positive thoughts, events, and outcomes. It is a catalyst which sparks extraordinary results.

If you have a **Positive Attitude** and strive to give your best effort, you will overcome the immediate problems and find that you are ready for greater challenges.

The number one thing that produces a successful outcome for any project is a **Positive Attitude**.

Advantages of having a *Positive Attitude*:
1. Others will follow your lead.
2. It gives you the ability to change as needed.
3. Failure is never an option.

A thought to ponder: The difference between a great day and a bad day is attitude.

On a scale of 1 to 10, 10 being perfect, I give myself a: _____

I have read, understand, and believe the points as outlined for the personal trait of having a *Positive Attitude*.

_____   _____
Signature   Date

Personal thoughts regarding
the Trait of having a *Positive Attitude*

Why I gave myself this point value:

_____

_____

_____

_____

_____

_____

_____

What I can do to raise my point value:

_____

_____

_____

_____

_____

_____

_____

Why I believe this trait is important to have in my life:

_____

_____

_____

_____

_____

_____

_____

The Personal Trait of having a
Sense of Humor

"No, I'm not trying to fly. I just discovered that I have two hands."

Anyone is a lot more attractive when they have a *Sense of Humor.*

Every time you are able to find some humor in a difficult situation, you win. A person without a *Sense of Humor* is like a car without shocks—you feel every small bump in the road.

A good *Sense of Humor* is an escape valve for the pressures of life. Through humor, you can soften some of the worst blows that life delivers, and once you find laughter, no matter how tough or painful the situation, you can survive.

A *Sense of Humor* is part of the art of leadership, getting along with people, and getting things done.

A *Sense of Humor* is the pole that adds balance to our steps as we walk the tightrope of life. You have to have a *Sense of Humor* to keep your sanity.

A *Sense of Humor,* as with some of the other traits, needs to be controlled. You see, others are not always in a very good mood.

If you could choose just one characteristic to get you through life, choose a *Sense of Humor.*

Advantages of having a *Sense of Humor*:
1. You are instantly more attractive.
2. People enjoy being around you.

3. People with a good **Sense of Humor** have a better sense of life.

A thought to ponder: You certainly can go through life without a **Sense of Humor,** but it will be a very long, hard road.

On a scale of 1 to 10, 10 being perfect, I give myself a: _____

I have read, understand, and believe the points as outlined for the personal trait of having a **Sense of Humor.**

_____   _____
          Signature   Date

Personal thoughts regarding
the Trait of having a **Sense of Humor**

Why I gave myself this point value:

_____
_____
_____
_____
_____
_____
_____

What I can do to raise my point value:

_____
_____
_____
_____
_____
_____
_____

Why I believe this trait is important to have in my life:

_____
_____
_____
_____
_____
_____
_____

Chapter 2

Employee Traits

Hard Worker
Goal Oriented
Ambitious
Personal Responsibility
Team Player
Self-Starter
Productive
Punctual

The Employee Trait of being a
Hard Worker

"I get great reviews, because I know what's expected of me, and I do it."

A **Hard-Working** employee is one who makes the most of his time, and who consistently produces good work.

A **Hard-Working** employee exhibits the traits of productivity, motivation, dedication, and self-reliance.

A **Hard-Working** employee stays focused on the tasks before him and spends little time chatting with other employees.

You will not catch **Hard-Working** employees browsing the Internet for personal information. They are ethically motivated to provide an honest day's work for their wages and take pride in their accomplishments.

Hard Workers are motivated to do the best job they can. They eagerly look forward to any training that might help them do better, and are the first to volunteer for new projects. **Hard Workers** consistently produce work of acceptable-to-excellent quality, and they look for more work when everything assigned to them is completed.

Hard Workers do not require constant supervision, and are self-reliant and accurate. They do not need hand-holding, but are not afraid to ask for help or additional training if needed. They are reliable, and consistently meet deadlines and production goals.

Hard Workers are dedicated to their employers, which makes them an asset to their companies.

Advantages of being a *Hard Worker*:
1. You are respected by your employer.
2. You may be rewarded with a higher income.
3. You will feel a great sense of accomplishment.

A thought to ponder: It is much easier to be a *Hard Worker* than it is to work hard at getting out of work.

On a scale of 1 to 10, 10 being perfect, I give myself a: _____

I have read, understand, and believe the points as outlined for the employee trait of being a *Hard Worker*.

_____   _____
Signature   Date

Personal thoughts regarding
the Trait of being a **Hard Worker**

Why I gave myself this point value:

_____
_____
_____
_____
_____
_____
_____

What I can do to raise my point value:

_____
_____
_____
_____
_____
_____
_____

Why I believe this trait is important to have in my life:

_____
_____
_____
_____
_____
_____
_____

The Employee Trait of being
Goal Oriented

"Mr. Jones, I invited you to my office to let you know that another raise is coming your way. You have again exceeded your goal."

When you believe that you can accomplish something, you are halfway there.

To achieve a goal you must first define it, want it, believe it, write it down, split it up into manageable parts, review it, establish a time frame, and make it happen.

There's a difference between interests and goals. When you have an interest in doing something, you do it only when it's convenient. However, when it's a true goal, you make no excuses and settle for nothing but positive results.

First, determine what you want and why you want it. Once you understand what's really important, your passion will get you there. Goals are accomplished by those who are consistent. They keep their eyes on the goal, as if they were wearing blinders, letting nothing distract them from achieving their objective.

When you are on the bottom, keep your goal firmly in view, and you will find renewed energy to continue the climb. *Goal Oriented* people are connected with action and continue to move; they may make mistakes, but they never quit. Every goal and every accomplishment starts with the decision to try. The only way one can fail is to stop trying.

Achieving a goal is not nearly as important as the person you become by doing so.

Advantages of being *Goal Oriented*:
1. You are known as one who never quits.
2. You wake up every day with a purpose to life.
3. You know that obstacles are not the end but are simply distractions.

A thought to ponder: Whether you believe you can accomplish a goal or you believe you can't, you will always be right.

On a scale of 1 to 10, 10 being perfect, I give myself a: _____

I have read, understand, and believe the points as outlined for the employee trait of being *Goal Oriented.*

_____   _____
           Signature   Date

Personal thoughts regarding
the Trait of being *Goal Oriented*

Why I gave myself this point value:

_____

_____

_____

_____

_____

_____

_____

What I can do to raise my point value:

_____

_____

_____

_____

_____

_____

_____

Why I believe this trait is important to have in my life:

_____

_____

_____

_____

_____

_____

_____

The Employee Trait of being
Ambitious

"I can tell you, Mr. Jones, you set a great example for your fellow employees when it comes to **Ambition**."

Ambition is wanting something you've never had and knowing that in order to obtain it, you must do something that you have never done. **Ambition** is always the road to success, and hard work will be the vehicle with which to travel. **Ambition** is the ability to put your fears behind you and your goals and dreams in front of you.

Ambitions are dreams—with a plan to make them a reality. Rewards are given to those who have **Ambitions**. **Ambitions** take you toward the good things in life and away from the bad.

Ambition is aiming high, moving forward; it's understanding that goals are not accomplished by wishful thinking but by having a plan for success. **Ambition** can overcome other things, like inexperience. Anyone with time will gain experience, but **Ambition** cannot be taught.

Ambition releases our unlimited potential. Everyone has the ability to make the impossible possible. There is no one that can hold an **Ambitious** person down for a long period of time. When good habits and perseverance meet with **Ambition**, the end result is always victory.

Advantages of being *Ambitious*:
1. You're known for not needing constant supervision.
2. You cannot be easily distracted.
3. You are known for being goal-oriented.

A thought to ponder: A person's worth is no greater than his or her **Ambition**.

On a scale of 1 to 10, 10 being perfect, I give myself a: _____

I have read, understand, and believe the points as outlined for the employee trait of being **Ambitious**.

_____   _____

           Signature   Date

Personal thoughts regarding
the Trait of being *Ambitious*

Why I gave myself this point value:

_____
_____
_____
_____
_____
_____
_____

What I can do to raise my point value:

_____
_____
_____
_____
_____
_____
_____

Why I believe this trait is important to have in my life:

_____
_____
_____
_____
_____
_____
_____

The Employee Trait of taking
Personal Responsibility

"Mr. Jones, I don't have to tell you that none of us are perfect. I do, however, want to let you know that I really respect you for never blaming others and always taking *Personal Responsibility*."

Accepting **Responsibility** is knowing that it's you, and you alone, driving the car of your life. It's you, and you alone, who determines the right and left turns in your life. **Personal Responsibility** is not only recognizing the errors of our ways, but having the will and ability to correct them.

Personal Responsibility is not a one-time deal, but a lifestyle. The choices we make daily ultimately shape our lives. Once you acknowledge and take **Personal Responsibility** for yourself, you are well on your way to making the necessary changes that will transform your life.

Circumstances such as where you were born, who your parents are, the year of your birth, and even your gender, are fixed. However, you can change yourself by taking **Personal Responsibility**.

The best day of your life is the day that you realize you are in complete control, and that by taking **Personal Responsibility**, you have the opportunity to become all that you can be. By taking **Personal Responsibility**, you can make all of your dreams become a reality.

Remember that you are always responsible for what you say and how you act, no matter how you may feel.

Advantages of taking *Personal Responsibility*:
1. You will feel great about your accomplishments.
2. You will be known for never blaming others.
3. Others will enjoy working with you.

A thought to ponder: No one ever brought positive change to themselves by blaming someone else.

On a scale of 1 to 10, 10 being perfect, I give myself a: _____

I have read, understand, and believe the points as outlined for the employee trait of taking *Personal Responsibility*.

_____   _____
         Signature   Date

Personal thoughts regarding
the Trait of taking *Personal Responsibility*

Why I gave myself this point value:

_____

_____

_____

_____

_____

_____

_____

What I can do to raise my point value:

_____

_____

_____

_____

_____

_____

_____

Why I believe this trait is important to have in my life:

_____

_____

_____

_____

_____

_____

_____

The Employee Trait of being a
Team Player

"Mr. Jones, I have to say, you exhibit skills in working with others that I seldom see. You must have played team sports in college."

Being a *Team Player* is understanding that there are always views other than your own. A *Team Player* makes others the focal point, listens intently, praises freely, and takes the spotlight off him- or herself.

Being a *Team Player* is one of the best contributions anyone can bring to a company. If a company is to reach its true potential, each employee must be willing to put aside his or her personal agenda for the good of the company.

A *Team Player*, always doing his or her best, becomes a natural leader just by example. Good employees inspire themselves, while great employees inspire others and earn promotions.

In business, coming together is a start; staying together is called progress; working as a team is called success. The achievements of any company are the results of the combined efforts of the individuals working together toward one common goal.

Working alone, we can accomplish little, but working as a team, the company can be taken to the top, whereby all are rewarded.

Advantages of being a *Team Player*:
    1. **Team Players** are truly appreciated by employers.

2. They are compensated, in part, on their ability to get along with others.
3. They are held in high esteem by other employees.

A thought to ponder: Nothing secures your future like being a *Team Player*.

On a scale of 1 to 10, 10 being perfect, I give myself a: ____

I have read, understand, and believe the points as outlined for the employee trait of being a *Team Player*.

_____   _____
              Signature   Date

Personal thoughts regarding
the Trait of being a *Team Player*

Why I gave myself this point value:

_____
_____
_____
_____
_____
_____
_____

What I can do to raise my point value:

_____
_____
_____
_____
_____
_____
_____

Why I believe this trait is important to have in my life:

_____
_____
_____
_____
_____
_____
_____

The Employee Trait of being a
Self-Starter

"As an employee, I realize that time does not stand still. Therefore, I don't stand around waiting for you to tell me that it's time to go to work."

Self-Starters jumpstart new projects, wrap up unfinished business, set and meet deadlines, and create and fulfill goals. *Self-Starters* are those who obtain greatness. They believe in their companies as well as themselves, and they follow their dreams. People at the top are there because they chose to be *Self-Starters*.

Good things come to those who obtain employment; better things come to those who work hard; and the best things come to those who work hard and are also *Self-Starters*.

In order to be irreplaceable, one must be different and bring value to a company. Being a *Self-Starter* does just that. No one ever lost his or her job by being a *Self-Starter*.

A *Self-Starter* is the one who holds the key that drives the engine of success. The strongest factor for success is being a *Self-Starter*, believing you can accomplish what you start, and believing that you deserve it.

Be a *Self-Starter* and do your best. It might just be all you really need.

Advantages of being a *Self-Starter*:
1. *Self-Starters* are respected and appreciated by employers.
2. They accomplish their goals in less time.
3. They are known for getting things done.

A thought to ponder: An employed person who has to constantly wait for direction will soon become unemployed, while an unemployed *Self-Starter* will soon become employed.

On a scale of 1 to 10, 10 being perfect, I give myself a: ____

I have read, understand, and believe the points as outlined for the employee trait of being a *Self-Starter*.

_____   _____
Signature   Date

Personal thoughts regarding
the Trait of being a *Self-Starter*

Why I gave myself this point value:

_____
_____
_____
_____
_____
_____
_____

What I can do to raise my point value:

_____
_____
_____
_____
_____
_____
_____

Why I believe this trait is important to have in my life:

_____
_____
_____
_____
_____
_____
_____

The Employee Trait of being
Productive

"Sir, there's one thing that I know for sure. If I don't produce a profit for this company, it's just a matter of time before I will be looking for a new job."

Being **Productive** means to start now. When you start now, instead of tomorrow, you will always finish a day sooner.

I like for things to happen, and I know that they will not happen on their own. That's why I'm always taking steps to make them happen.

Being **Productive** is not an accident. It's when excellence, intelligent planning, and focused effort come together. **Productive** people make no excuses, waste no time, and have no regrets.

The goal of employment is not simply to collect a paycheck, but to matter, to be **Productive**, to be useful, and to make a positive difference. I realize that I am not paid for being busy, but for being **Productive**.

People who are **Productive** are promoted. They don't ask what the company can do for them, but what they can do for the company. The question is not "How can I become the best *in* the company?" but "How can I become the best *for* the company?"

You must remain **Productive** and focused on your journey to greatness.

Advantages of being *Productive*:
1. Goals are accomplished.
2. Promotions are obtained.

3. A **Productive** person is known for not being a procrastinator.

A thought to ponder: *Productive* people start where they are, use what they have, and do what they can.

On a scale of 1 to 10, 10 being perfect, I give myself a: _____

I have read, understand, and believe the points as outlined for the employee trait of being **Productive**.

_____   _____
       Signature   Date

Personal thoughts regarding
the Trait of being *Productive*

Why I gave myself this point value:

_____
_____
_____
_____
_____
_____
_____

What I can do to raise my point value:

_____
_____
_____
_____
_____
_____
_____

Why I believe this trait is important to have in my life:

_____
_____
_____
_____
_____
_____
_____

The Employee Trait of being
Punctual

"Mr. Jones, I would like for you to know that you will be recognized for *Punctuality* at this year's employee banquet. You will receive an award for not being late for work one day within the last five years. You will also find a nice surprise in this week's paycheck."

Punctuality is a form of politeness; it's a sign that you are not above others and that you appreciate the opportunity that you have been given. *Punctuality* is more valuable than money. You can get more money, but you cannot get more time. Arriving late is a way of saying that your own time is more valuable than the time of the person who is waiting for you.

Punctuality is a choice. Employers know that *Punctual* employees will make good choices in other aspects of their jobs. Successful people are *Punctual*; they have order in their lives and are diligent in what they do. *Punctual* people have a determination that leads to success.

Preparedness and *Punctuality* are two of the most important qualities a leader can possess.

Procrastination and *Punctuality* are both habits. Procrastination is keeping up with yesterday, while *Punctuality* is keeping up with today. Which one will you choose?

Perhaps *Punctuality* is even more valuable because it is found in so few people. May it be found in you.

Advantages of being *Punctual*:
1. People know that you are dependable.

2. You provide a great example for others.
3. You will be judged by what you do more than by what you say.

A thought to ponder: If you wouldn't be late in picking up your pay check, then don't be late in earning it.

On a scale of 1 to 10, 10 being perfect, I give myself a: _____

I have read, understand, and believe the points as outlined for the employee trait of being *Punctual*.

_____   _____
Signature   Date

Personal thoughts regarding
the Trait of being *Punctual*

Why I gave myself this point value:

_____
_____
_____
_____
_____
_____
_____

What I can do to raise my point value:

_____
_____
_____
_____
_____
_____
_____

Why I believe this trait is important to have in my life:

_____
_____
_____
_____
_____
_____
_____

Chapter 3
Leadership Traits

Taking Ownership
Confident
Even-Tempered/Calm
Concern for Others
Leading by Example
Good Listener
Planning for Success
Persistence

The Leadership Trait of
Taking Ownership

"Good Morning. I've called this meeting with the three of you so that I might commend each of you for the outstanding ways in which you have been representing this company. All three of you accept feedback gladly and never make excuses. As a result of your outstanding performances, each of you will receive a bonus."

Taking Ownership is accepting responsibility, being accountable, and understanding that you are in complete control of your own destiny. *Taking Ownership* is having a strategy, purpose, vision, and willingness to make and accept change when necessary.

People who *Take Ownership* understand that they must never stop learning, because life is forever teaching. People who *Take Ownership* recognize a problem, make a plan, take action, and get results. They are just crazy enough to believe that they can take a company to a new level, and guess what? They can.

Always say what you mean and mean what you say, because the one who minds doesn't matter, and the one who matters will appreciate it.

Today is my opportunity to shape tomorrow, take control, and make positive things happen. How good tomorrow will be is determined largely by the choices I make today.

Seize the moment and make the most of it, for an entire day is made of moments. People who *Take Ownership* accomplish more in a short period of time than others could ever imagine.

Advantages of *Taking Ownership*:
1. Your boss will not be looking over your shoulder.
2. You will feel great about your accomplishments.
3. You will be trusted with important company projects.

A thought to ponder: Rather than relying on others, ***Taking Ownership*** puts you in charge of your own destiny.

On a scale of 1 to 10, 10 being perfect, I give myself a: _____

I have read, understand, and believe the points as outlined for the leadership trait of ***Taking Ownership***.

_____   _____
Signature   Date

Personal thoughts regarding
the Trait of *Taking Ownership*

Why I gave myself this point value:

_____

_____

_____

_____

_____

_____

_____

What I can do to raise my point value:

_____

_____

_____

_____

_____

_____

_____

Why I believe this trait is important to have in my life:

_____

_____

_____

_____

_____

_____

_____

The Leadership Trait of being
Confident

"I would like to thank each of you for taking time away from your families to attend this special, called meeting. I would like to apologize if I come across as arrogant. The fact is, I have **Confidence** and know that I can take this company to a new level. The good news for you three is that I'm going to take you with me."

Confidence is knowing that the results will be remarkable before even one step has been taken. **Confidence** takes preparation: it's laying a solid foundation, having a plan, and having all the necessary tools to complete the project. Everything else is beyond one's control.

What lies behind and before a person is nothing compared to what lies *inside* a person with **Confidence**. Every time a person fails, they can gain **Confidence**, knowing that the world doesn't end. The fact is, we enjoy our successes, but we learn much more from our failures.

Most people believe that the grass is always greener in someone else's backyard. A person with **Confidence** does not buy into this myth, and knows that it's all about fertilizing the grass he or she is standing on.

Everyone has limitations. When we listen to our critics, their limitations become ours. When we have **Confidence**, we are in complete control and determine our own limitations.

Splendid things are only accomplished by those who dare to believe that they can overcome the same circumstances that the others around them face.

Advantages of being *Confident*:
1. People will follow and trust in your abilities.
2. Employers will provide you with additional responsibilities.
3. Others know that you are not afraid to change directions.

A thought to ponder: A person can grow only as much as his or her vision will allow.

On a scale of 1 to 10, 10 being perfect, I give myself a: _____

I have read, understand, and believe the points as outlined for the leadership trait of being **Confident**.

_____   _____
            Signature   Date

Personal thoughts regarding
the Trait of being **Confident**

Why I gave myself this point value:

_____
_____
_____
_____
_____
_____
_____

What I can do to raise my point value:

_____
_____
_____
_____
_____
_____
_____

Why I believe this trait is important to have in my life:

_____
_____
_____
_____
_____
_____
_____

The Leadership Trait of being
Even Tempered/Calm

"I believe that we all understand that in order to become a leader with this company or any company, having a calm demeanor in difficult situations is of utmost importance."

Being **Even Tempered** is having the ability to control one's emotions in the midst of a storm. Being **Even Tempered** is being free from excitement. It is holding agitations within. It's maintaining tranquility and serenity in difficult situations.

Even Tempered people are calm, composed, cool-headed, peaceful, serene, unruffled, and unexcitable.

One of the biggest factors that hold people back from becoming good leaders is that they speak without understanding or considering what the outcome will be.

Not being calm and giving in to anger allows others to control your emotions. All people get angry from time to time. **Even Tempered** people get angry at the right person, to the right degree, at the right time, for the right reason, and in the right way.

Always be slow to anger and even slower to speak when you are angry; taking words back is like trying to get toothpaste back into the tube.

Advantages of being *Even Tempered/Calm*:
1. People enjoy working with and for you.
2. People will treat you with the respect you deserve.
3. Your **Even Tempered** demeanor will be contagious.

A thought to ponder: You can never win by losing your temper.

On a scale of 1 to 10, 10 being perfect, I give myself a: ____

I have read, understand, and believe the points as outlined for the leadership trait of being **Even Tempered/Calm**.

_____   _____

            Signature   Date

Personal thoughts regarding
the Trait of being *Even Tempered/Calm*

Why I gave myself this point value:

_____
_____
_____
_____
_____
_____
_____

What I can do to raise my point value:

_____
_____
_____
_____
_____
_____
_____

Why I believe this trait is important to have in my life:

_____
_____
_____
_____
_____
_____
_____

The Leadership Trait of showing
Concern for Others

"Mary, you are correct. People will only follow your lead if they know that you have their best interest at heart."

Showing **Concern for Others** is understanding that the only way you can become successful is to assist others in obtaining their success.

Showing **Concern for Others** is asking a simple question like "What can I do to help you have a better day?" or "What can I do to help you with the project you are working on?"

Showing **Concern for Others** is like making a deposit in their bank; at some future point, it will come back to you with interest. No one will ever respect a person who does not first have concern for them.

One of the best ways you can show your **Concern for Others** is to be a good listener. It's very difficult to understand how to help someone unless they tell you where they need help. A few minutes of listening to someone will eliminate hours of guessing what their needs may be.

Never underestimate the value and impact of a smile, a kind word, or an honest compliment. When you care more for others than they believe is necessary, the results you'll receive will be far more than others will expect.

Showing **Concern for Others** is a sign of strength, not weakness.

Advantages of showing Concern for Others:
1. Friends will be easily obtained.

2. People will gladly follow your lead.
3. People will always be willing to do you favors.

A thought to ponder: Never be too busy to show *Concern for Others*.

On a scale of 1 to 10, 10 being perfect, I give myself a: _____

I have read, understand, and believe the points as outlined for the leadership trait of showing *Concern for Others*.

_____   _____
         Signature   Date

Personal thoughts regarding
the Trait of showing *Concern for Others*

Why I gave myself this point value:

_____
_____
_____
_____
_____
_____
_____

What I can do to raise my point value:

_____
_____
_____
_____
_____
_____
_____

Why I believe this trait is important to have in my life:

_____
_____
_____
_____
_____
_____
_____

The Leadership Trait of
Leading by Example

"The first thing that I want all of you to know is this: If you are going to be leaders with this company, you need to fully understand that people are far more impressed by what you do than what you say."

Leading by Example is not putting greatness into people but getting the best out of people—because they want to give you their best.

Leading by Example is having the ability to assign people to positions for which they are suited, letting them know that you believe in them, and then trusting them to do the job.

Leading by Example is to walk and work beside others, using the word *we*, rather than *I*.

Leading by Example is not just another thing that influences others—it's the only thing. More than what you say, it's what you do that impacts others.

Leading by Example is empowering others to greatness. When *Leading by Example* you inspire others to learn more, do more, and wish to accomplish more. If your actions inspire others to dream more, learn more, do more, and become more, you are indeed a leader.

Leading by Example isn't just another way to teach, it's the only way. A good example has much more value than good advice. *Leading by Example* is saying what you mean and meaning what you say.

Advantages of *Leading by Example*:
1. People are willing to follow your lead.

2. The people you supervise will be very productive.
3. You will be appreciated and rewarded by upper management.

A thought to ponder: People know you for what you've done, not for what you plan to do.

On a scale of 1 to 10, 10 being perfect, I give myself a: _____

I have read, understand, and believe the points as outlined for the leadership trait of *Leading by Example*.

_____   _____
Signature   Date

Personal thoughts regarding
the Trait of *Leading by Example*

Why I gave myself this point value:

_____

_____

_____

_____

_____

_____

_____

What I can do to raise my point value:

_____

_____

_____

_____

_____

_____

_____

Why I believe this trait is important to have in my life:

_____

_____

_____

_____

_____

_____

_____

The Leadership Trait of being a
Good Listener

"We all need to understand that we were given two ears and one mouth for a reason."

Being a **Good Listener** is the number one way to show that you are truly concerned for the other person's welfare.

Being a **Good Listener** means keeping your body still and your eyes focused on the one who is speaking.

Being a **Good Listener** means sitting quietly, paying attention, not interrupting, and waiting for your turn to speak. You can learn much by listening and nothing by talking. Your undivided attention has a great value to others; it also shows that they have value to you.

A great conversation is always made up of two **Good Listener**. It's impossible to respond to another in a concerned way if you haven't heard a word they said.

Being a **Good Listener** is a way of letting others know that they, and what they have to say, matter to you. Encouraging them to talk about themselves will build respect.

A **Good Listener** listens with the primary intent of understanding, and the secondary intent of replying.

Being a **Good Listener** involves *hearing, sensing, interpreting, evaluating,* and then *responding.*

Advantages of being a Good Listener:
1. Others will open up to you more freely.
2. You will learn much about those around you.

3. You will understand what upper-management expects of you.

A thought to ponder: All great leaders are *Good Listeners.*

On a scale of 1 to 10, 10 being perfect, I give myself a: ____

I have read, understand, and believe the points as outlined for the leadership trait of being a *Good Listener.*

_____   _____

Signature   Date

Personal thoughts regarding
the Trait of being a *Good Listener*

Why I gave myself this point value:

_____
_____
_____
_____
_____
_____
_____

What I can do to raise my point value:

_____
_____
_____
_____
_____
_____
_____

Why I believe this trait is important to have in my life:

_____
_____
_____
_____
_____
_____
_____

The Leadership Trait of
Planning for Success

"**Planning for Success** is having a strategy that allows you to visualize the end before you start."

Planning for Success is defining your objective and understanding the process. It involves teamwork and staying focused until the goal has been accomplished.

Planning for Success means not allowing the circumstances of today to distract from the goals of tomorrow.

When *Planning for Success,* make sure that you have all necessary resources in place prior to execution.

Planning for Success is knowing where you're going, how you're getting there, and when you're arriving.

Planning for Success starts with a vision and ends with a job well-done.

Planning for Success is the ability to break down a job into manageable parts. It's not getting overwhelmed.

There are worthy goals and ambitious goals, but the goals that get accomplished faster are the ones that start with a plan for success. *Planning for Success* provides a strategy that aligns with business objectives and drives improved performance.

Spending the proper time planning means you will spend less time making corrections.

Advantages of *Planning for Success*:
1. Others will follow your lead.
2. Accomplishing your goals will become routine.

3. You will be respected by those with whom you work.

A thought to ponder: If you don't know where you're going, you might just end up someplace else.

On a scale of 1 to 10, 10 being perfect, I give myself a: ____

I have read, understand, and believe the points as outlined for the leadership trait of *Planning for Success*.

_____   _____

      Signature   Date

Personal thoughts regarding
the Trait of *Planning for Success*

Why I gave myself this point value:

_____

_____

_____

_____

_____

_____

What I can do to raise my point value:

_____

_____

_____

_____

_____

_____

Why I believe this trait is important to have in my life:

_____

_____

_____

_____

_____

_____

The Leadership Trait of having
Persistence

"It's vital for all of you to understand that the key to success is ambition, but what will get you to the goal line is being **Persistent**."

Any goal worth starting is worth completing. When you think that you can't go on, force yourself. Success is based on **Persistence**, not luck. **Persistence** is the key. Never stop trying and eventually you will accomplish what others simply dream about.

Winning or accomplishing one's goal is a combination of drive and **Persistence**. The desire to make another effort or try another approach is the secret to success. Accomplishing any worthwhile goal is never easy, but it is always worth it.

Patience, **Persistence**, and hard word are an unbeatable formula for success. Remember, a river will cut through stone, not because of its power, but because of its **Persistence**.

Everyone fails, but with **Persistence,** failure becomes postponed success. Victory is never far away when one has the habit of **Persistency**. There are no shortcuts or secrets to success. It's simply a result of having a vision, hard work, and the **Persistence** to get the job done.

Ideas are a dime a dozen. The **Persistence** to see the idea through to completion is priceless.

Advantages of having *Persistence*:
 1.   You'll be known as one who never gives up.

2. Others will love to follow your lead to the finish line.
3. You will often be recognized for jobs well done.

A thought to ponder: Everything in life that's worth having is worth working for.

On a scale of 1 to 10, 10 being perfect, I give myself a: _____

I have read, understand, and believe the points as outlined for the leadership trait of having **Persistence**.

_____   _____

Signature   Date

Personal thoughts regarding
the Trait of having *Persistence*

Why I gave myself this point value:

_____

_____

_____

_____

_____

_____

_____

What I can do to raise my point value:

_____

_____

_____

_____

_____

_____

_____

Why I believe this trait is important to have in my life:

_____

_____

_____

_____

_____

_____

_____

Chapter 4
Family Traits

Generous
Understanding Sowing
Non-Judgmental
Faithful
Trustworthy
Good Money Manager
Respect for Others
Thoughtful

The Family Trait of being

Generous

"As a family we get great satisfaction from doing things for those who can never pay us back. We believe it's a great lesson to teach our children."

Generosity is giving unselfishly to others, to those in need, and to those less fortunate. It means sharing not only financial resources but also time and talents.

We should never forget that happiness, joy, and contentment do not come from obtaining something that we don't have, but in providing for others' needs.

Real *Generosity* is giving when you yourself are in need, realizing that the one you give to is in greater need.

Opportunities to help the multitude may never come, but people in need will forever be with us.

Generosity is more than giving money. It's also giving your time. *Generosity* is speaking a kind word to someone who has been rude to you, not because they deserve it, but because it's the right thing to do.

True relationships are based on trust, honesty, and *Generosity*. The greatest single quality for any family member is to show love. Yes, it's the ability to share one's love and time, and yes, that is true *Generosity*.

When you see an opportunity to help, do so. You can never be *Generous* too soon, because you never know how soon it will be too late. We make a living by what we earn, but we make a life by what we give back.

Advantages of being *Generous*:
1. Others will know that you are not motivated by materialism.
2. You will have an inner peace and contented life.
3. Others will acknowledge your loving and giving ways.

A thought to ponder: A person's wealth is measured not by fame or fortune, but by what they give back.

On a scale of 1 to 10, 10 being perfect, I give myself a: _____

I have read, understand, and believe the points as outlined for the family trait of being ***Generous***.

_____   _____

Signature   Date

Personal thoughts regarding
the Trait of being **Generous**

Why I gave myself this point value:

_____

_____

_____

_____

_____

_____

_____

What I can do to raise my point value:

_____

_____

_____

_____

_____

_____

_____

Why I believe this trait is important to have in my life:

_____

_____

_____

_____

_____

_____

_____

The Family Trait of
Understanding Sowing

"We are a very happy family because we know that our happiness comes from giving to others. The most important thing that we understand and teach our children is to give love and respect to other family members."

Sowing and reaping is a simple concept: what you send out comes back; what you sow, you reap; what you give, you get; and what you see in others exists in yourself.

Understanding Sowing is realizing that if you do not have what you need or want, you should take a close look at the quality of the seeds you are sowing. Inferior seeds produce an inferior product. Sowing good seeds of love, joy, peace, patience, goodness, kindness, and generosity will generate a great harvest of loving relationships.

The seeds you sow will determine if your harvest will be flowers or weeds. Give away at least ten percent of your earnings, and the balance will be much more enjoyable. When sowing, don't expect instant results. Remember, the farmer plants in one season, and harvests in a different season.

Be a giver of what you would like to receive from others. If you wish to be loved, be loving. If you wish for honesty, be honest. If you wish for respect, be respectful.

Don't judge your days by the harvest you reap. Rather, keep sowing and know that the harvest is on its way. Never be surprised if you harvest a lot more than you sow; a good harvest far exceeds that which was planted.

Advantages of *Understanding Sowing*:
1. People will appreciate the seeds that you sow in their lives.
2. Others will, in turn, plant seeds in your life.
3. You will have a calm and loving family and work environment.

A thought to ponder: It's impossible to harvest a good crop without sowing good seeds.

On a scale of 1 to 10, 10 being perfect, I give myself a: ____

I have read, understand, and believe the points as outlined for the family trait of ***Understanding Sowing***.

_____   _____
            Signature   Date

Personal thoughts regarding
the Trait of **Understanding Sowing**

Why I gave myself this point value:

_____
_____
_____
_____
_____
_____
_____

What I can do to raise my point value:

_____
_____
_____
_____
_____
_____
_____

Why I believe this trait is important to have in my life:

_____
_____
_____
_____
_____
_____
_____

The Family Trait of being
Non-Judgmental

"I believe that as a family member it's very important that one is **Non-Judgmental**, instead attempts to put themselves in the shoes of the other person. We need to understand that there's a reason behind what everyone does or says."

We all have imperfections in our lives that could be improved. Therefore, do not judge others for their imperfections that are smaller than your own. For everyone, life is a journey of becoming a better person.

Trying to understand the issues in the lives of others is far more valuable and productive than wasting time being judgmental. Never judge someone for what they look like. What's on the inside is of greater importance.

When we spend time judging others, it leaves less time to judge the only one over whom we have control. To judge others is to assume that you know which road in life they are taking. When we are judgmental of others, it does not define who they are but who we are.

It is always better to forgive than to judge. Life is very simple when we treat others the way that we would like to be treated.

Everyone needs to accept the things in life that cannot be changed, the courage to change the things they can, and the wisdom to know the difference.

If you don't like judgmental people, then don't be one.

Advantages of being *Non-Judgmental*:
1.   People will confide in you.

2. You will have a large number of close friends.
3. You will be respected and loved by family members as well as friends.

A thought to ponder: Anyone looking for friends without faults will have no friends.

On a scale of 1 to 10, 10 being perfect, I give myself a: _____

I have read, understand, and believe the points as outlined for the family trait of being **Non-Judgmental**.

_____   _____
Signature   Date

Personal thoughts regarding
the Trait of being **Non-Judgmental**

Why I gave myself this point value:

_____

_____

_____

_____

_____

_____

_____

What I can do to raise my point value:

_____

_____

_____

_____

_____

_____

_____

Why I believe this trait is important to have in my life:

_____

_____

_____

_____

_____

_____

_____

The Family Trait of being
Faithful

"As a father and husband, I understand that the best example I can set for my children is to be a loving and *Faithful* husband to their mother."

Being *Faithful* is never a sacrifice, but is always a sign of true love. There is no greater treasure than a *Faithful* spouse or friend.

In marriage, we say *I do*, but what it really means is *I will*— I will love you regardless, I will be truly devoted regardless, and I will be *Faithful* regardless. Choosing to love, respect, and be *Faithful* to only one woman, are all qualities of a real man.

Being *Faithful* means never having to look back and wonder what happened to your relationship or your marriage. Real men and women stay *Faithful* because they don't have time to look for partners. They are too busy loving their own.

There is no such thing as being *somewhat* *Faithful*, you are either *Faithful* all the time or you are simply unfaithful. In any relationship, *Faithfulness* is never an option but always a priority.

Faithfulness is the key to inner peace, joy, and a happy and fulfilling life. *Faithfulness* is understanding that the grass is never greener, and that what makes grass green is fertilizing what you're standing on.

Being *Faithful* extends beyond the family to all relationships, including that between an employee and an employer.

Advantages of being *Faithful*:
1. People will know that you are trustworthy.
2. You have a much better chance of being in a long-lasting, loyal, and loving relationship.
3. ***Faithfulness*** carries over to friends, coworkers, and those in authority.

A thought to ponder: If you can't stay ***Faithful,*** stay single, as an unfaithful spouse has little value.

On a scale of 1 to 10, 10 being perfect, I give myself a: ____

I have read, understand, and believe the points as outlined for the family trait of being ***Faithful***.

_____   _____

       Signature   Date

Personal thoughts regarding
the Trait of being *Faithful*

Why I gave myself this point value:

_____
_____
_____
_____
_____
_____
_____

What I can do to raise my point value:

_____
_____
_____
_____
_____
_____
_____

Why I believe this trait is important to have in my life:

_____
_____
_____
_____
_____
_____
_____

The Family Trait of being
Trustworthy

"As a mother and especially as a wife, I know that the reason we have such a great marriage is because my husband is completely **Trustworthy**. Being **Trustworthy** in our marriage has always been a two-way street; it applies to both of us. Everyone needs to know that you can't have love without first having **Trust**."

Trustworthiness is priceless. Many wealthy people have left their spouses to be with poor people that they could trust. **Trustworthiness** is the key that opens the door to every successful relationship.

Trust is the foundation, the essential ingredient, and the bonding glue with which all great relationships are built. Real and long-lasting marriages are not based on sex, romance, large homes, fancy cars, or big screen TVs but are based on respect, compromise, and **Trust**.

Being **Trustworthy** is a trait that takes years to build and seconds to destroy—requiring a lifetime to repair.

Four things that you can never recover in life: a stone after it's thrown, a word after it's spoken, time after it's gone, and trust that has been lost. **Trust** can be like a mirror that was broken and repaired; every time you look in it you can't help but see the cracks.

In relationships, respect is earned, honesty is appreciated, **Trust** is then gained, and loyalty is returned. The best compliment anyone can give you is to say, "I **Trust** you." Don't ever make someone regret saying that to you.

Advantages of being *Trustworthy*:
1. Others will know that your word is your bond.
2. Others will not be afraid to share personal information with you.
3. Your relationships of all kinds will be built on a strong foundation.

A thought to ponder: *Trustworthiness* is the foundation of simply saying what you mean and meaning what you say.

On a scale of 1 to 10, 10 being perfect, I give myself a: _____

I have read, understand, and believe the points as outlined for the family trait of being ***Trustworthy*.**

Signature	Date

Personal thoughts regarding
the Trait of being *Trustworthy*

Why I gave myself this point value:

_____
_____
_____
_____
_____
_____
_____

What I can do to raise my point value:

_____
_____
_____
_____
_____
_____
_____

Why I believe this trait is important to have in my life:

_____
_____
_____
_____
_____
_____
_____

The Family Trait of being a
Good Money Manager

"As a father and husband, not only do I have to be a hard worker in order to support and provide for my family, but we have to set money aside each and every week to make sure that our future will be as bright as our present."

Being a *Good Money Manager* starts by not spending money that you don't have on things you don't need. The key to a successful life is simply: When you stop buying items you don't need, you have more time and money to enjoy the real things that matter—and that's each other.

Good Money Management is very simple: Either you control it, or it controls you. Three out every five Americans do not track their expenses. If you don't have a plan for moving forward, in all likelihood you will move backward.

Money is only a means to the end; your reason for making money should always be of greater value than the money itself. Ultimately, it's not what you earn that will determine your success, but what you save.

All money you save goes toward making your future more secure. All money you spend on things you don't need goes toward securing someone else's future.

Living a contented and stress-free life is knowing that you are well prepared for rainy days, and at the same time are making a difference. Helping others is one of the best investments you will ever make.

Be sure of why you're working, because success is just the beginning. The real value, happiness, lies in enjoying what you have.

Advantages of being a *Good Money Manager*:
1. There will be little financial stress in your life.
2. You will have great credit scores.
3. You will have funds to take advantage of good investment opportunities.

A thought to ponder: If you would be embarrassed for others to review your check book expenditures, then you may need to work on your money management.

On a scale of 1 to 10, 10 being perfect, I give myself a: _____

I have read, understand, and believe the points as outlined for the family trait of being a *Good Money Manager*.

_____   _____
Signature   Date

Personal thoughts regarding
the Trait of being a **Good Money Manager**

Why I gave myself this point value:

_____

_____

_____

_____

_____

_____

_____

What I can do to raise my point value:

_____

_____

_____

_____

_____

_____

_____

Why I believe this trait is important to have in my life:

_____

_____

_____

_____

_____

_____

_____

The Family Trait of showing
Respect for Others

"As husband and wife we have a tremendous **Respect** for each other. We understand that being a good person does not depend on religion, status in life, race, or skin color. Good and decent people always treat others with **Respect**."

Respecting Others starts with **Respecting** yourself. You can never give away something that you don't have. **Respect Others** even if they don't respect you, and never allow anyone to determine how you feel about yourself.

Respect is a very simple concept: it's treating others the way you would want them to treat you. This one little reality, if practiced by all, would completely eliminate bullying in schools and families, as well as the workplace. Never underestimate the power of **Respecting Others**. **Respecting** someone costs nothing but will add great value to them. Even a smile may allow someone to have a brighter day.

It is not important that you like or dislike a person, but it is important that you **Respect** each one as a human being. People are different; no two people have the same life experiences. No two people share the same realities of life, but everyone needs to continue to learn and to be respected. **Respect** the wrong, the weak, and the elderly—because at some point you will be all three.

You don't need to know someone well in order to show **Respect**. Remember that everyone is fighting their own battles. Everyone has personal problems that they are attempting to solve. Out of all that humans' desire, 95 percent of them are the same as yours. Never disrespect a person because of the five percent that makes him or her different. **Respecting Others** is a form of sowing; it's giving what you would like to receive. Love, honesty, and **Respect** are all things that everyone would like to receive. Give and you get in return.

Advantages of showing *Respect for Others:*
1. People will **Respect** you.
2. Others will admire and confide in you.
3. Other will give you the benefit of the doubt.

A thought to ponder: *Respect* cannot be demanded but is reserved for those who deserve it.

On a scale of 1 to 10, 10 being perfect, I give myself a: _____

I have read, understand, and believe the points as outlined for the family trait of showing **Respect for Others**.

_____   _____
Signature   Date

Personal thoughts regarding
the Trait of showing *Respect for Others*

Why I gave myself this point value:

_____
_____
_____
_____
_____
_____
_____

What I can do to raise my point value:

_____
_____
_____
_____
_____
_____
_____

Why I believe this trait is important to have in my life:

_____
_____
_____
_____
_____
_____
_____

The Family Trait of being
Thoughtful

"We both fully understand that being **Thoughtful** costs very little and sometimes nothing. It's simply understanding the little things in life that mean so much to the person you love. My wife doesn't wish for a new car, as a tender shoulder rubbing will do just fine. As for me, I enjoy fishing, and my wife enjoys me having that pleasure when I can."

Thoughtfulness is the number-one way to show that love is not just a word but an action.

Feeling that you should show an act of **Thoughtfulness** and not following through is like wrapping a present and leaving it in the closet. There is never a gift too small to give when wrapped in love, with a bow of **Thoughtfulness** on top.

Showing **Thoughtfulness** is making love to someone's heart. The most romantic and loving gifts always come from the heart, not the wallet. Often, giving your time can be a great gift of **Thoughtfulness**. Strong and lasting relationships are always made up of **Thoughtful** gifts along the way.

People who wish to show concern can use words. People who really care let their actions do the talking.

Being **Thoughtful** is seeing through the eyes of others, hearing through the ears of others, and feeling through the hearts of others.

Advantages of being *Thoughtful*:
1. You will have strong loving relationships.

2. Home will be a place of peace and calmness.
3. You will be rewarded and honored with love and respect.

A thought to ponder: Being *Thoughtful* will fill an empty glass.

On a scale of 1 to 10, 10 being perfect, I give myself a: _____

I have read, understand, and believe the points as outlined for the family trait of being *Thoughtful*.

_____   _____
            Signature   Date

Personal thoughts regarding
the Trait of being **Thoughtful**

Why I gave myself this point value:

_____
_____
_____
_____
_____
_____
_____

What I can do to raise my point value:

_____
_____
_____
_____
_____
_____
_____

Why I believe this trait is important to have in my life:

_____
_____
_____
_____
_____
_____
_____

Notes:

_____
_____
_____
_____
_____
_____
_____
_____
_____
_____
_____
_____
_____
_____
_____
_____
_____
_____
_____
_____
_____
_____
_____
_____
_____
_____
_____
_____
_____
_____

Traits the Poster

The poster, measuring 2' by 3', is designed
for both classrooms and businesses.
The poster is designed, not only be a constant
reminder for students as well as employees, but to
also make a powerful statement to customers.

Trait
What every employer is looking for

Personal Traits
Integrity
Honesty
Humility
Patience
Self-Control
Correct Motives
Positive Attitude
Sense of Humor

Employee Traits
Hard Worker
Goal Oriented
Ambitious
Personal Responsibility
Team Player
Self-Starter
Productive
Punctual

Leadership Traits
Takes Ownership
Confident
Even Tempered/Calm
Concern for Others
Leads by Example
A Good Listener
Plans for Success
Persistent

Family Traits
Generous
Understands Sowing
Non-Judgmental
Faithful
Trustworthy
Good Money Manager
Respect for Others
Thoughtful

For more information and to purchase
both books and posters please visit
WWW.TRAITSTHEBOOK.COM